This illustrated novel is written in the first-person voice of the main character, Amy Millison, and she tells of her experiences in school, and at home.

Amy takes her readers on an adventure in this book and we see what kind of life a child her age, in a new school environment goes through. The book is a simple story that should engage the target audience very easily. Kudos to Dara Oginni for this book and hoping more lovely children's books are coming from this young, amazing author.

*Sinmisola Ogúnyinka, Author, Blue Dawn.*

# SCHOOL FRIENDSHIP SOLUTIONS

## New school, New friends

Dara Oginni

Matador
9 Priory Business Park,
Wistow Road, Kibworth Beauchamp,
Leicestershire. LE8 0RX
Tel: 0116 279 2299
Email: books@troubador.co.uk
Web: www.troubador.co.uk/matador
Twitter: @matadorbooks

ISBN 978 1800461 871

British Library Cataloguing in Publication Data.
A catalogue record for this book is available from the British Library.

Typeset in 13pt Blambot FXPro Light BB by Troubador Publishing Ltd, Leicester, UK

Matador is an imprint of Troubador Publishing Ltd

flower book series

To my family,

Thanks for helping me
with this book.

# Prologue

Welcome to Amy's new life! Amy has started a new school, but nobody there bothered to say, "Hi, what's your name?" and her greatest enemy there is Sapphire. You think she's super nice, don't you? Well, no. She's not! Let's see what happens...

# Chapter One

# NEW SCHOOL

Hi there! Welcome to my life. My name is Amy Millison. I have a mum, dad and a little sister called... *Dingdong! Dingdong!* Oh, wait a minute; I have to get ready for my new school. I gotta go.

Anyway, my sister's name is Ellie!

I had to leave all the mess in my bedroom, rush downstairs and then pounce on the table, where my toast and chocolate spread was already served. Ellie, my little sister, was already eating. She always goes downstairs to eat in her pyjamas.

Ten minutes later, I arrived at school. Luckily, I was just in time. I ran to the classroom (Year 5a). I put my jumper in the cloakroom, put my bags away and found a seat... On my own.

It was time for the register. Our teacher, Miss Siller, called out, "Hello, Year 5a, welcome to your classroom."

"Good morning, Miss Siller," everyone replied grumpily.

"The register starts now. Harry."

# "Yes."

"Everest."

"Toby."

"yes."

"Yes."

"Milly, no playing with Everleigh's hair."

"Yes, Miss."

"Ayomi."

"Everleigh."

"Yes."

"Naomi."

"Yes."

"Yes."

"Keira."

"Jade."

"Yes."

"Yes."

"Matthew."

"Yes."

"Last but not least, Sapphire."

"Ooh! Don't forget Kelly and Sivanthi!"

"Yass."

"Yes!"

"Yes!"

What? My name was not on the register! Well, what a GOOD start. I called out, "Umm... excuse me, Miss, am I in the wrong class? My name's Amy. Amy Millison." I heard another person, it must have been a girl, whisper, "What an ugly name," but I ignored it and kept focused.

Miss Siller scanned the register and nodded. "Sorry, Emeline, wait, is that your name? Or is it Amy? Even though your full name is Amelia, I can call you Amy, right?" I nodded on the outside, but on the inside, I sighed, distraught. This was going to be a LONG year.

"So today," carried on Miss Siller, "we are going to do some maths. After Mr Johnson's lesson tomorrow, you are going to have a test. So concentrate – if you get C or lower, you will get detention."

"What, huh?" the classroom stammered, but I am ninety-nine per cent sure I heard the same girl say, "Yeah, well, whatever – I won't break a sweat getting an A." Anyways, we'll leave that snooty girl and go back to me. I knew, I just knew, I would get double detention! I needed to study hard.

# So much embarrassment!

The school day was soon over. Then I went home, changed to some other clothes and I went to do my homework. It took me an hour. Ellie came into the room. She is so embarrassing.

Ellie innocently told me that we were going to
the park so I should change into something
better for the weather. "Come on! I have to change
again!" I said under my breath.

Ellie sweetly said, "Well, we have to do what
Mummy says!" I lunged towards her, then tackled
her to the ground. Unfortunately for me, that was
the exact moment Mum came in to see me.
That was the end of that.

At the park, you would not be able to guess who we met: Kelly, Sivanthi and Sapphire. I was so amazed and pleased – I was like, "Hi, Kelly, hi, Sivanthi, hi, Sapphire. Do you wanna hang out with us?"

Sapphire said, "Excuse me, with you? Even my dog, Fifi, who drinks out of the toilet, hated your ugly, cheap, second-hand shirt!" I'm guessing THAT was a no.

Kelly and Sivanthi had different replies. They said, "Sure." Kelly and Sivanthi are so nice – they can be my BFFs! Sapphire is so rude – she can be my enemy! We ran around, chatting and giggling about my first embarrassing details of when I first joined the school. Sapphire was getting jealous. She tripped me over and I fell into the dustbin! (YEAH, SERIOUSLY!) ☹☹☹

That's when I made my first enemy. My nickname for Sapphire is Rudiron. You get the point? Not? Well, the point is that it rhymes (kinda), she's rude and when she is rude her face looks hot and red like an iron! I know, right?! I can't believe that she pushed me into the dustbin. A few seconds later, Kelly and Sivanthi rushed to me and quickly helped me up.

"Are you OK?" asked Sivanthi.

"Yes," I said, my cheeks glazing like the scorching sun, brushing the slimy, rotten, smelly banana peels off my shirt.

"I like your denim skirt," said Kelly.

"Thanks, it's new," I replied.

# Got an enemy and two BFFS.

Good morning! (Really it's a bad morning.) Did you have a good night? I am so scared! I have a test today! It's maths! I suck at maths! Remember what Miss Siller said yesterday? (If not, read her instructions above all over again.) I am in school right now and the register has just finished.

"So today, I hope you succeed in your test," said Miss Siller. "It's a fifteen-minute test with thirty questions. Don't worry, they are very basic. Do your best! No cheating!" She eyed at some of the boys, supposedly the troublemakers, then looked, smiling warmly, back at the class. *What?* I thought. *It usually takes me an hour!*

While I was doing the test, I figured out (after a lot of working out – not maths questions, BTW) that if Sapphire is the rude one, she probably said those things in class! "Stop!" said Miss Siller. "Time is up! You may put your pencils down."

*Oh no!* The test had finished and I'd only done... four questions! Well, at least I worked something very IMPORTANT out.

"D?!" *Nooo!* I hoped this was a dream; I closed my eyes and pinched myself very hard, but no, it wasn't a dream. Miss Siller said I have to help clean the toilets. Yuck! Eww!

I got detention and I had to clean the toilets. What a welcome to a new school!

Not long after, school was then over and I was back home. I called, "Mum, are you home?" Nobody answered. "Dad, are you home?" Nobody answered. There was no point in calling Ellie – she's only four and she can't stay at home by herself. So I ran up to my bedroom and lay down on my bed, crying. Wait for five minutes, please.

Soon enough, Mum, Dad and Ellie all came. "Honey, we are home!" shouted Mum. I ignored her; seconds later she came into my room. "There you are, darling," she said. "We all went to the meadow to have a picnic."

I said in my head, *We all! WE ALL! Urr, I'm clearly not part of this family, then!* "We should all have gone on that picnic!" I replied, agitated.

Dad wanted to change the conversation to something more joyful. "Ellie made a puppet called Penny because she was made by a pen." Dad chuckled.

## A lovely day off school.

Woo hoo! It's the weekend! Mum says I can go to Kelly's house. Sivanthi's coming too. Let's go!

Wow! Kelly's house is beautiful. There are marble tables, a beautiful chandelier and their kitchen is the size of our living room. TIMES TWO! Wow, the garden is filled with flowers, such as pansies, marigolds and roses. The lush green grass is beautifully trimmed and... no way! A bench! I brought my purple and blue diary and pen.

"Hi, Sivanthi, how are you?"

"I am very well, thank you," replied Sivanthi, kindly.

"Hi, guys." Jumping in, Kelly turned to me. "Sorry about the detention yesterday – next time study a little bit harder. Like, really hard. So hard you go to bed at seven!"

"OK, I'll keep that in mind," I said.
"Now let's go and play!"

"I have a puppy called Toffee. She's a cocker spaniel.
A gorgeous chocolate brown one. Do you want to
play with her?" Kelly asked. "Don't worry, Sivanthi,
she's really sweet." She laughed, seeing Sivanthi's
worried face.

We played with the adorable little cutie with the most
golden-brown fur and big, cute eyes.

# Chapter Two

# ELLIE TIME

Welcome back to Amy's world. Amy is planning to go to her BFF, Sivanthi's house, but Mum has other plans.

Yay! Perfect, I am going to look after my sister Ellie!
Woohoo! NOT! I wonder what MISCHIEF she might get
into?! I will be in so much trouble! Here is a list of
what she might do:

* Ruin my favourite blue and purple T-shirt
  (AGAIN! – It already has ink blotches).

* Cut off some of my hair.

* Use Mum's beauty products.

* Call the police because I didn't let her
  have Doritos and pickles for breakfast or
  use the house phone.

* Eat all of Dad's peanut butter and jelly
  sandwich which he was saving for later.

* RUIN her princessy doll which Mum bought
  for £50!

* Have a wrestling match with my baby
  brother Jameson's blankie thingy (and rip
  it up!).

Those are the reasons why I am reaaalllllyy worried
about babysitting her. So now you know what
mischief she probably will get into.

Like, OMG! You have to help me! I am so frustrated!

So what do I do now?
I might as well play on my iPad or listen to music on
my dad's iPod... NOT! I'll do both.

So now I'll go up to my room. Bye!

"Eliana Brianna Eleanor Millison!
What are you doing?! You scared my heart out of me!
Why are you dressed as a bunny?"

"First things first," she said, "I told you not to call
me by my full name, Eliana! You did! 'Cos you got
cooties! Would you like it if I called you Amelia?!
Anyways, Mummy said I could dress up as a bunny
and then come to you."

"Why did she say that?"

"Um... because I... said I wanted to give
you a nice surprise!"

"Can I do my part of the story, Amelia Nikki Jamie
Millison? On that ugly looking blurple – (blurple is
what Eliana – I mean, ELLIE – calls blue and purple; it
actually is a nice word!) – diary of yours? It should
be a sparkly pink if you ask me!"

"OK, I get it! On the next page, though." Who does Miss 'Blurple is an ugly colour!' think she is?

"Yay! Thanks, AMELIA!"

I scowled. How many times do I have to tell her to call me Amy?! "I will get ready."

Ellie's side of the story

OK, Ellie, your handwriting is sloppy, you have lots of spelling mistakes, and you bent and tattered the pages. I couldn't even read the third page! Time for bed! It's nearly nine!

---

1    Sorry about her bad spelling and grammar. (Even I can do better than that! What is she doing in her school?)

2    I had to change most of the spellings, but I left the BEST ones.

I woke up in bed, startled. I had the worst dreams
ever! But only one of them could wake me up.

So Sapphire, what she did in my dream,
scared me. Anyway, it's morning – I'll wake Ellie up.
Before I do, did you have a good night? Write your
dream here. Or draw.

"Good morning, Ellie, dear sister.
Wake up, wake up! Rise and shine."

"Is it time yet?" she grumbled. "Five more minutes."

"No!" I moaned. "Mum said we should
get up at eight o'clock and it's 8:30!"

"Fine! You win!" she said as she stuck
her tongue out at me. "Fine! Meanie!"

"You will be sorry soon, Ellie!"
I shot back at her. "You will!"

"I will not!"

I didn't want to get another fight going
so I just said, "Okay, you won't."

"Ha ha ha. I win, you lose."

"Come on, let's get ready for the day,"
I said, ignoring the things Ellie said.

Ellie and I totally rockin' it in our outfits.

Oh, I forgot to tell you. We are going to the mall.
Since we have been good (Ellie's good is finishing
HALF of her food and mine is doing all my chores,
emptying and filling the dishwasher, cleaning my
room, etc.), Mum said we can buy what we want with
£10 each. We are going after breakfast. I can't wait.
We are having sausages, beans and toast. Delicious!
We gotta go. *Thump, thump, thump,* we descend the
stairs. Yum, I can't wait to eat. Since the mall is
around the corner and there are lots of safe adults
we know, we can go by ourselves.

OK, bye, Mum. Let's go to the mall.


Good times.

I guess it wasn't that bad after all
(my half term with Ellie).

# Chapter Three

# I WANT A PUPPY!

# Part 1

Will I get one?

Hi again! It's so nice to see you.

I really want a puppy, but my mum won't let me have one until I'm eighteen. I am only nine now, so I will need to wait another nine years! It's so unfair.

Anyway, how's your day? Do you have a pet?

I've had hundreds of dog toys, but Ellie (my naughty little sister) broke them all. (Do not ask how!) So I am stuck without what I really want. I want a golden retriever – they're so sweet and bouncy. I hope my mum and dad get me a puppy, but really there IS NO CHANCE of that happening. Oh no! I just remembered that I need to tidy my bedroom! Oh no! Right now! My mum is going to be angry – so much for chores! Gotta go. Bye!

*Thump! Thump! Thump! Thump!* Phew, I am here, not there. I'm sure the mess can't be THAT bad. I am a tidy person, after all.

This tidying up is going to take forever; I better get started now. This is what it looks like now. A MESS! You know what, it's also time for bed. Tomorrow is a school day. I can't wait to see my BFFs, Kelly and Sivanthi. Oh, I better sleep. I have a long day in front of me. Tomorrow we are going to be in pairs for swimming safety. You might think it will be fun, but I can't swim! Ellie is confidently swimming in the advanced class with people over TWICE her age, while I'm nervously wading around in the Tiny Turtles class, which is for toddlers! I hope I go with Sivanthi or Kelly, so swimming won't be as bad! Anyways, good night to you. This is how my very strange day began.

Oh no, I am late! AGAIN!

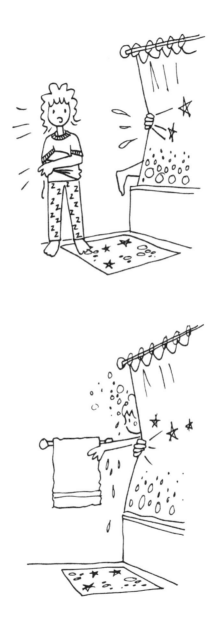

OMG! What... How fast was I?
OK, now I gotta go. It probably took me two minutes
fifteen seconds! I'm gonna go in the car – I don't
wanna be late for school.

OK, I am here, finally.
I'm just gonna go to class and...

"Amy!" cried Sivanthi and Kelly. "You're here."

"Hi, guys," I said as we did a group hug.

What a lucky friend I am.

"Come on, we have to get to the swimming class,"
cried Sivanthi. "I can't wait to swim."

"Same here," cheered on Kelly.

"Yes," I grumbled. "Let's go." (I guess I know why they're excited to swim. They are both really good and go to a proper club. Just because THEY'RE excited about it doesn't mean I have to be.)

But before we could move, Rudiron (Sapphire) came. This is what she said: "Oh, so it's my favourite losers: Amy, Sivanthi and Kelly. How's ya losin'? I'm sure you've lost your integrity, wearing those outfits. Who made them? The tooth fairy?!"

"Um, I think you are the one who is losing. Losing your MIND!" Kelly replied, standing up for us.

"Listen, you pipsqueaks!" Rudiron hissed. "You better stay outta my hair before I call Mrs Cherry – (the principal) – on you! Take my advice, or you'll be sorry!" Remembering that Sapphire has a poodle, Fifi, made me want a dog even more.

35

You should have seen it – some kids were calling me a snitch and just to leave people alone. Was I the snitch? NU UH! She was. They were literally standing up for Sapphire. Luckily, the teacher came and made the class so quiet that you could hear a pin drop. Then Sapphire said in her sweetest voice, "Excuse me, Mrs Clark. I will tell you that Amy will be really rude in the future and very snobby."

This is what I wanted to do:

This is what I did:

# Chapter Four

# I WANT A PUPPY!

# Part 2

...I am so sad! I stood there for half an hour, sulking!
At first, I thought this would happen...

Sapphire and I as BFFs,
but unfortunately it looks like this...

I know, the pictures of Sapphire look totally different. What! OMG! Swimming class! I just remembered! I mean, I just forgot! I gotta go!

Phew! I'm here – I better go and change.

"Miss Millison! You are late! We are just about to start! Now get into your swimming costume!"

Oh no, that was our swimming teacher, Mr Ale. Wait... did I leave the house with my swimming bag? ...Ellie distracted me this morning by asking me to buy a baby unicorn from the supermarket with my £2.50 pocket money... and... NO! I remember! I left it on the landing today! How could I? "Err, Mr Ale, I don't have my um... my, um... swimming suit!"

"Oh, then you will have to wear this..." He trailed off, holding up the six-year-old-sized embarrassment (clearly wanting everybody to see it!). Sapphire snorted pompously and wrinkled her nose, while she was looking nice in her cute, sparkly aquamarine and turquoise wave-coloured bikini that looked like it cost quite a lot of money. Yes, a lot to say, huh?

Anyways, back to me. "Oh, not that!" I muttered, referring to the swimming costume that Kelly showed me earlier.

"You're gonna have to push a lot because the swimming suit's really wet an' tight..." he carried on.

Urrr! I really wished I had brought my own!

"Get in it!" Mr Ale shouted. "The swimming suit."

"OK," I grumpily muttered.

"Speak up!" he barked.

"OK, sheesh!" By stupidly opening my big mouth I got detention for the SECOND time in just two weeks. Just great! *Ow! Squelch! Bang! Crash! Ow! Squelch!* Finally!

"OK, so we are going to be doing swimming pairs for swimming safety," said Mr Ale, then he stated all the pairs: Kelly and Sivanthi, Sapphire and Amy. No! Even Sapphire looked glum too (of course she would, am I silly?!). So did Kelly and Sivanthi.

"OK, so, Sapphire, you are a lifeguard on that chair and you see a girl drowning, waving her arms out in a panic – what would you do?"

"Well, let me see," said Sapphire. "Oh, I would just sit there and watch, let her save herself! DIH! Do It Herself! Has the skunk ever heard of it?!" All the other kids laughed so hard at her joke; I almost laughed too!

POOL DEPTH 1.0m

Mr Ale blew his whistle, and it was so quiet
after that. "Get serious!" he shouted.

"OK!" said Sapphire, hurriedly.
"I'd save her from the water, Mr Ale."

Mr Ale nodded approvingly and said,
"OK, Amy, get in the water... It isn't deep, only
0.9..." I took a cautious step forward, then, *splash!*
Sapphire pushed me in! Let me drown, please.

POOL DEPTH 1.0m

School's over. I guess I had a WONDERFUL DAY!

"You're here," said Dad cheerfully.
"Where have you been?"

"Detention," I muttered, blinking back tears,
ruining the joyful mood.

"Oh, well," sighed Dad. "Try and behave, A.
We don't want any letters from the school.
This will surely brighten your spirits.
Come and open this, you will like it."

"No way!" I sighed, happily. A puppy!

"Oh my goodness!" squealed Ellie. "A puppy?
I have always wanted a puppy forever."

"You girls had been talking about dogs nonstop all week; it made me seriously consider getting one. And, something told me that dog was the right one!"

I narrowed my eyes at him. Now, what did THAT little comment mean? Had they been hiding the puppy from us all this while?

"Amy," said Dad. "Remember half term, when Mum asked you to take care of Ellie? That wasn't just for nothing. It was to see if you were responsible enough for a puppy! You did such a good job, and if you can take care of a JOB like Ellie, you sure can take care of a puppy."

Wow, Dad finally admitted Ellie was a job! That did brighten my spirits! (About Dad saying that nice thing about me, not him calling Ellie a job.)

"What should we name her?" asks Mum. When she looked at our confused faces she said, "Yes, she's a she."

"Daisy Rose!" Ellie and I said in unison.

"Then Daisy Rose it is," replied Dad.

Welcome, our newest Millison family member, Daisy Rose. Yay! Hooray!

"Two whole days of puppy fun!" I squealed.

"Best day ever!" said Ellie.

"These are all the things we bought for her online. We thought they were really nice," replied Mum. "But remember; this is extremely important – this mainly goes to you, Ellie. NO feeding Daisy food off the table! She will ONLY eat her dog food from Waggy Tails! Some food, like chocolate and grapes, are poisonous to dogs!" I gotta keep that in mind.

"Wow," I breathed. "Daisy's gonna love this!"

"Let's take a picture of Daisy Rose," suggested Mum.

This is how to look after golden retrievers:

* Develop a feeding schedule.

* Provide plenty of clean, fresh water.

* Provide some healthy treats.

* Avoid giving your golden retriever human foods as it can be poisonous to them.

* Bond with them and make friends as quickly as you can!

BTW, I found everything easy, but the feeding schedule is pretty difficult. I mean, I have horse-riding lessons with Sivanthi and Kelly every Thursday after the eighth session. For some unknown reason that is the day that Daisy R is most hungry. Major fail! Plus, she is a very fussy eater. Can you believe it?

HOORAY FOR DAISY ROSE!

"Girls," said Dad. "Daisy will sleep in your rooms, in alternating days. On Monday, Amy. Tuesday, Ellie. Wednesday, Amy. Thursday, Ellie. Friday, Amy. Saturday, Ellie and on Sunday, she will sleep my room."

You probably don't know this, but I write everything that's going on in my life in my diary, my blue and purple one. I even write in it at school, only when we have a half-an-hour break when you can go get some snacks and drinks from the vending machine between third and fourth session. At lunch I'm too bouncy to write. I usually wanna play tag with Kelly and Sivanthi.

I have lots of puppy-proofing to do,
now that Daisy is here. I'd probably bore
you with all the stuff, so I'm gonna skip that.
This will take A LONG TIME. So, see ya!

## Chapter Five

# GIRLS' DAY OUT

Amy is going to the mall and to find out why
Sapphire is so mean to everyone. But, wait, what if
her mall day is ruined and she just makes Sapphire
even meaner! She needs a friend to be with her or
help. Or two!

Hi, guys! Can you be quiet? It's maths class and I'm writing in my notebook. I'm rushing – that's why it isn't my best handwriting. (If I get caught, it'll be another detention for me! This school is so STRICT.) Look at Sapphire's big, black barrette in her hair! It kinda looks a bit strange... wait a sec... Eww! There is a bug in Sapphire's hair! I better get it out for her. Not that I should. She would think I put it there.

"Get it out! I don't want two nasty bugs in my hair. Get it out!" cried Sapphire. I was like, *Sorry, sis, I'm not a nasty bug – maybe you might turn into one, 'cos you got one in your hair. Common sense, girl; use it! So sorry! I forgot, you ain't got any!* I just said that in my head, so no one heard it but me.

Calling Sapphire a mean girl is an UNDERSTATEMENT!
She's a ticked-off bull in three coats of lip gloss,
hair extensions and hoop earrings!

"Amy," called the teacher. "Your parents want you to
go home now. So pack your things and go, please..."
She trailed off, looking towards the other kids, with
a stern glare that could freeze them. S and K gave
me warm smiles and jazz hands. I do not deserve
friends like these!

What? Are my parents angry or cross with me for
something? Surely the time when I nearly burnt
down the house baking cookies last Christmas has
been put behind us! Or the time when I accidentally
cracked Mum's new expensive vase, playing tennis!
Or the time when... OK, you get it. I have been in lots
of SITUATIONS before! I walked home...

And then...

"Amy! Welcome your new big sister, Nikki!
And your little sister, Holly!"

"My new sisters! What? Why do we have new sisters?
That's impossible!"

"We adopted them," said Dad.

"Hi," said Nikki, my big sister. "You must be Amy. Ellie
told me about you. She said you had hairy legs and
crusty eye boogers," she said, wrinkling her nose.

How dare she talk about me like that!
'She' meaning Ellie, not Nikki. "Awwww," I said.
"Holly looks so cute! Can I carry her?"

"Of course you can," said Mum.
So I picked her up and...

I will tell you about Nikki. She has my second name
and she looooves sports and animals, like me; she
is a brunette, like the rest of us, except Holly and
Dad. She is five point two feet tall and her hobbies
are babysitting, violin playing and sports. She
absolutely loves all of them! Holly is so cute and
loves her baby bottle and pacifier. She loves teddies
and cute things; that's why she loves Daisy Rose.
She absolutely adores my old teddy, Nibbles. BTW,
Holly and Dad have black hair. Oh! I forgot to tell
you! Nikki and Holly come from Florida! So lucky! I still

have to get used to their accent.
I have a little baby brother who is even younger
than Holly. His name is Jameson. We call him
James for short. He is only a few months old
and sleeps and eats and cries... yeah, so boring.
He was my little brother from the start,
but I don't really talk about him much.
He is usually at home when I get back from
school at 3:45. He is really cute, though.

I went back to school and it was break time, so I
went outside...

And...

That guy is SUPER COOL (maybe he can help me with
maths!)! I wonder what Sapphire thinks about him!

Anyway, a few hours passed
and I am at home now... Doing...

Then...

"Coming, Mum!" I grunted. How could she interupt me when I am writing in my diary? (BTW, I don't think I spelled interrupt right. Hey, don't laugh! We haven't learnt it in our spellings yet!) I trudged downstairs for ages.

Then I saw Kelly and Sivanthi on the computer. Sivanthi said, "Hi, Amy; we were wondering if you could–"

"Let me take it from here," Kelly interrupted. "Go to the mall with us!"

I asked my mum and she replied with a yes! SQUEEE! OMG! Yay! WOOHOO!

I can't believe I am going to the mall with Sivanthi and Kelly! I have to go and change into something nice and trendy... Boom!

Tada!

Ellie asked, "Can I come to the mall with you?"

Then she whined, "Nikki! Amy won't let me go to the mall with her!" (You can guess what my answer was.) Yes, a big, fat NO.

My mum sighed and said, "If you want to go without me, you have to go with Nikki and Ellie. I'll keep Holly and James at home." All I wanted to say then was...

Great! Anyway, Kelly and Sivanthi came.

I said, "Hey! I thought you going
to see me at the mall!"

"Yeah," replied Kelly, "but we thought you
weren't coming, so we came here to yell at
you for not accepting... Oww!"

Sivanthi gave her a swift kick to shut her up.

"How did you get here?" I asked.

"Simple," replied Sivanthi,
"we live just round the corner."

"Oh, OK, anyway, meet my big sister
Nikki and my little sister Holly!"

"Nikki," I said, "put some shoes on and a jacket. Time to go! Bye, Mum. Bye, Dad!" I have to admit, walking to the mall is not so fun. I know, I know, during the half term with Ellie, I said it wasn't far from our house, but walking takes a long time, doesn't it? BTW, we need to get going!

Write how long it would take you to walk to the mall.

On the way, we were like, totally gossiping about school friend solutions and how so many girls have come to ask us for advice. You know, I actually never knew our club could get so popular. Here is a popularity chart (my friends and I, we're the bottom three of most unpopular). I'm last, Kelly second last and Sivanthi third last.

| Most popular person | Most popular club |
|---|---|
| * Sapphire Harmony | * School friend solutions |
| * Michael Roberts (the new boy) | * Make-up girls |
| * Chloe Grey | * Strengthen your mind |
| * Tom Charleson | * Sport it up |
| * Maya Sabrines | * Be cool, dude! |

Finally! We are at the mall! So many shops!
What to buy? Where to go? As I took another
small step, I heard a sneer from one
familiar person...

S A P P H I R E

(My mouth was sooo wide open.)

There was Sapphire Senior,
Sapphire and Sapphire Junior.

I couldn't believe it. Sapphire never told me she had sisters! (Not that she would.) Sapphire said, "Meet my big sister Gemma and my little sister Crystal." (Gemma looked twice as unfriendly as Sapphire – also twice as mean – but Crystal looked really sweet!)

Gemma had a fake tan, blonde extensions (like Sapphire), fake eyelashes – everything like Sapphire: a black denim jacket, embroidered with diamonds! Sapphire looked exactly the same, just with a rose gold fluffy jacket that was sleeveless and, wait... her blouse said, 'sassy, remove the dorks'! (That gem was there too.) Anyways, she had a silver ruffled skirt that had purple gems on it. As for her sister, she had brown heeled boots that had purple gems on it. (Seriously, what is with the new craze of purple gems?) BTW Gemma's dress was turquoise, yellow and light pink. Crystal was really cute. She wore a rose gold fluffy jacket (is there a new craze again?!) that had sleeves and she had chocolate brown hair. Her blouse had a... oh no! A purple gem; she had a baby blue skirt on that was a darker blue on the top, purple tights and black Mary Jane shoes! Cute! Us party of friends just ignored the sassy divas while Ellie was screaming, "No! I want to say hi to Crystal!"

Anyways, we got on with the shopping; we went and bought loads of super cute tees, including a sparkly unicorn one for Ellie. Ellie also bought a tiara; S, K and I bought lip gloss. Nikki bought a new clear blue sequin case for her iPhone. Nikki also treated us to some cupcakes from the famous, oh-so-good, Cupcakie Craze!

Apparently, Crystal is best friends with Ellie from Rainbow Day Primary School. This was Ellie's face when I said she could talk to her.

One and a half hours later, we got back home; Kelly and Sivanthi went back to their own houses. I did my English and maths homework. Did you have any homework today? Write yes or no here.

**The nice dog (1)**

Amy Millison

1. What colour was the dog?
   Brown
2. What did he hurt?
   His knee
3. What did he do next?
   He spun around
4. Who was the author?
   Anna Welskins

**The nice dog (2)**

Amy Millison

The nice dog
The nice brown dog
Fell on a log
And hurt his little knee.

He spun around
Like a clown
And he was laughing
He He He

by Anna Watkins

**Arithmetic**

Amy Millison

1. $\sqrt{4} + \sqrt{4} = 4$
2. $12 \times 7 = 84$
3. $6 \times 9 = 54$
4. $4! = 24$
5. $5! - 4! = 5$

**Arithmetic**

Amy Millison

6. $0.1 + 3 = 3.1$
7. $82 + 5 = 87$
8. $87 + 56 = 143$
9. $\wedge = 4 + 5n = 9$
10. $3^3 = 27$

My Materials

Gtn, you got it!
★★★★

Then, trouble came – what was Ellie doing in my room? Like, what?! She asked if I could give her a hand. "With what?" I asked back.

She then said, "To SLAP you."

I was like, *Oh no, she didn't*,
so I ran after her – oh yeah, I did!

Then I decided to leave her and mark my homework. After all, she STILL is a little kid. I can't wait 'til she grows up! Her first step is to know that unicorns DON'T EXIST.

After that I was hungry,

Then I was so tired that I...

Goodnight.

The next day, when I got back to school,
the first thing I did at 8:45, before first session at
9:00, was run to the stables and grab my horse,
Phoenix. I tacked him up and mounted him;
Phoenix galloped to the school grounds for me
and then I shouted (NOT the horse), "SIVANTHI! KELLY!"

They slowly turned their heads round and said,
"AMY?"

I quickly dismounted and told them that we need to
get more attention to School Friendship Solutions;
girls need to know how to deal with friendships. But
the first so-called 'friendship' we needed to deal
with was with one particular girl: Sapphire. I put
Phoenix in the stables, trying not to let anybody
notice (again, if I was caught, it would be ANOTHER
detention for me!).

We surrounded Sapphire and asked, "Who are your
friends? Do you actually have any friends?"

Of course her answers were, "No, no," then she
burst into tears. She said the only reason she
wasn't the nicest to everyone (she admitted!) was
because nobody wanted to be her friend! After
everybody started being nice to her, they still
weren't her actual friends! She was really upset. So
we decided that if she was warm to us, she could be
our friend! She agreed, happily. Here comes the three
(I mean, FOUR) best friends, ready to have some fun!

And so we did.

THE END OF MY FIRST ENTRY! BYE! SEE YA IN THE NEXT ONE!

TOODLES!

flower book series

For exclusive discounts on Matador titles,
sign up to our occasional newsletter at
troubador.co.uk/bookshop